D0048205

Editor's Choice
2002

Fritz Luecke
Editorial Director

WEEKLY WR READER

This book belongs to:

For
mouah

WINNIE-THE-POOH
AND SOME BEES

A. A. MILNE

Winnie-the-Pooh and Some Bees

Adapted by Stephen Krensky

With decorations by
ERNEST H. SHEPARD

Dutton Children's Books
New York

This presentation copyright © 2001 by the Trustees of the Pooh Properties
From *Winnie-the-Pooh,* copyright © 1926 by E.P. Dutton & Co., Inc.;
copyright renewal 1954 by A. A. Milne.

Library of Congress Cataloging-in-Publication Data
Krensky, Stephen.
Winnie-the-Pooh and some bees / A. A. Milne; adapted by Stephen Krensky;
with decorations by Ernest H. Shepard.—1st ed.
p. cm.
Summary: Using a balloon to float in the air, Winnie-the-Pooh pretends
he is a cloud so that he can reach the bees' honey.
ISBN 0-525-46781-5 (hardcover)—ISBN 0-14-230041-1 (pbk.)
[1. Teddy bears—Fiction. 2. Toys—Fiction. 3. Bees—Fiction.] I. Shepard,
Ernest H. (Ernest Howard), 1879-1976, ill. II. Milne, A. A. (Alan Alexander),
1882-1956. III. Title.
PZ7.M64 Wi 2001
[E]—dc21   2001023927

Published in the United States 2001 by Dutton Children's Books,
a division of Penguin Putnam Books for Young Readers
345 Hudson Street, New York, New York 10014
www.penguinputnam.com

CONTENTS

1

POOH MAKES HIS FIRST APPEARANCE

Once upon a time,

a very long time ago now,

about last Friday,

Winnie-the-Pooh lived in a forest

under the name of Sanders.

One day when he was out walking,

he came to an open place

in the middle of the forest.

And in the middle of this place

was a large oak-tree.

From the top of the tree,

there came a loud buzzing-noise.

Winnie-the-Pooh began to think.

"That buzzing means something,"

he said to himself.

"You don't get a buzzing-noise like

that, just buzzing and buzzing,

without it meaning something."

"If there's a buzzing-noise,

somebody's making a buzzing-noise.

And the only reason

for making a buzzing-noise that I know of

is because you're a bee."

Then he thought another long time,

and said: "And the only reason

for being a bee that I know of

is making honey."

And then he got up, and said:

"And the only reason

for making honey

is so as *I* can eat it."

So he began to climb the tree.

He climbed and he climbed

and he climbed.

And as he climbed,

he sang a little song to himself:

Isn't it funny

How a bear likes honey?

Buzz! Buzz! Buzz!

I wonder why he does?

Then he climbed a little further…

and a little further…

and then just a little further.

By that time

he had thought of another song:

It's a very funny thought that,

   if Bears were Bees,

They'd build their nests

   at the bottom of trees.

And that being so

   (if the Bees were Bears),

We shouldn't have to climb

   up all these stairs.

He was getting rather tired now,

but he was nearly there.

And if he just stood on that branch…

Crack!

"Oh, help!" said Pooh,

dropping ten feet to the branch below him.

"If only I hadn't—" he said,

as he bounced twenty feet

on to the next branch.

"You see, what I meant to do—"

he explained,

as he turned head-over-heels

and crashed through

the next six branches.

Then he spun round three times

and flew gracefully into a gorse-bush.

"It all comes of liking honey so much,"

he said.

"Oh, help!"

He crawled out of the gorse-bush,

brushed the prickles from his nose,

and began to think again.

And the first person he thought of

was Christopher Robin.

2

POOH'S FUTURE
BECOMES CLOUDY

So Winnie-the-Pooh went round

to his friend Christopher Robin,

who lived behind a green door

in another part of the forest.

"Good morning, Christopher Robin," he said.

"Good morning, Winnie-the-Pooh."

"I wonder," said Pooh,

"if you've got such a thing

as a balloon about you?"

"A balloon? What do you want

a balloon for?"

Winnie-the-Pooh looked around

to see that nobody was listening.

"Honey!" he said in a deep whisper.

"But you don't get honey with balloons!"

said Christopher Robin.

"I do," said Pooh.

Christopher Robin had been

to a party the day before

at the house of his friend Piglet.

There had been balloons at the party.

He had brought a green one

and a blue one home with him.

"Which balloon would you like?"

Christopher Robin asked.

Pooh put his head between his paws

and thought very carefully.

"It's like this," he said.

"When you go after honey with a balloon,

the great thing is not to let

the bees know you're coming."

"Now, if you have a green balloon,

they might think you were part of the tree,

and not notice you.

And if you have a blue balloon,

they might think you were part of the sky,

and not notice you."

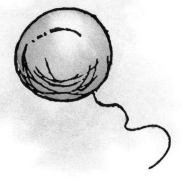

"Wouldn't they notice you

underneath the balloon?"

asked Christopher Robin.

"They might or they might not," said Pooh.

"You never can tell with bees."

He thought for a moment.

"I shall try to look like a small black cloud.

That will deceive them."

"Then you had better have

the blue balloon,"

said Christopher Robin.

And so it was decided.

They both went out with the blue balloon,

and Christopher Robin took

his gun with him, just in case.

And Winnie-the-Pooh went

to a very muddy place

and rolled and rolled and rolled

until he was black all over.

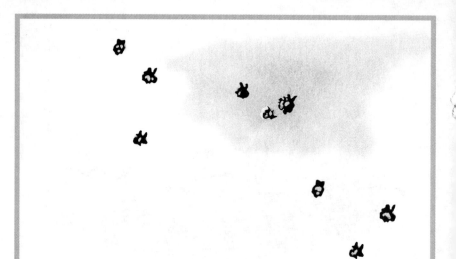

When the balloon was blown up

as big as big, Christopher Robin

and Pooh both held on to the string.

Then Christopher Robin let go suddenly,

and Pooh Bear floated up into the sky.

He stayed there—

level with the top of the tree

and about twenty feet away from it.

"Hooray!" shouted Christopher Robin.

"What do I look like?" Winnie-the-Pooh

shouted down to him.

"You look like a bear

holding on to a balloon,"

said Christopher Robin.

"Not—" said Pooh anxiously,

"——not like a small black cloud

in a blue sky?"

"Not very much."

"Perhaps from up here it looks different,"

said Pooh. "And, as I say,

you never can tell with bees."

There was no wind to blow him

nearer to the tree,

so there he stayed.

Pooh could see the honey.

He could smell the honey.

But he couldn't quite reach the honey.

3

POOH REFINES
HIS PLAN

After a little while he called down

to Christopher Robin.

"I think the bees suspect something,"

Pooh said in a loud whisper.

"What sort of thing?"

asked Christopher Robin.

"I don't know," said Pooh.

"But something tells me they're suspicious."

"Perhaps they think that

you're after their honey."

"It may be that," said Pooh.

"You never can tell with bees."

There was another little silence,

and then Pooh called down again.

"Christopher Robin!"

"Yes?"

"Have you an umbrella in your house?"

"I think so."

"I wish you would bring it out here,"

said Pooh. "I think, if you did that,

it would help with the bees."

So Christopher Robin went home

for his umbrella.

"Oh, there you are!"

called down Pooh when he got back.

"I have discovered that the bees

are now definitely Suspicious."

"Shall I put my umbrella up?"

said Christopher Robin.

"Yes," said Pooh,

"and walk up and down with it.

Then look up at me and say,

'Tut-tut, it looks like rain.'

I shall do what I can

by singing a little Cloud Song,

such as a cloud might sing."

So, while Christopher Robin

walked up and down

and wondered if it would rain,

Winnie-the-Pooh sang this song:

How sweet to be a Cloud

Floating in the Blue!

Every little cloud

Always *sings aloud.*

How sweet to be a Cloud

Floating in the Blue!

It makes him very proud

To be a little cloud.

4

POOH CHANGES
HIS MIND

The bees were still buzzing

as suspiciously as ever.

Some of them, indeed, left their nest

and flew all round the cloud

as it began the second verse of its song.

One bee even sat down

on the nose of the cloud for a moment,

and then got up again.

"Christopher—*ow!*—Robin,"

called out the cloud.

"Yes?"

"I have just been thinking, and I have come

to a very important decision.

These are the wrong sort of bees."

"Are they?"

"Quite the wrong sort," the cloud went on.

"So I should think they would make

the wrong sort of honey."

"Would they?"

"Yes. So I think I shall come down."

"How?" asked Christopher Robin.

Pooh hadn't thought about this.

If he let go of the string,

he would fall—*bump*—

and he didn't like the idea of that.

So he thought for a long time,

and then he said:

"Christopher Robin, just shoot the balloon

with your gun."

"But if I do that, I'll spoil the balloon."

"But if you don't," said Pooh,

"I shall have to let go.

And that would spoil *me*."

When Pooh put it like that,

Christopher Robin saw how it was.

He aimed very carefully at the

balloon—and fired.

"Ow!" said Pooh.

"Did I miss?" asked Christopher Robin.

"You didn't exactly miss," said Pooh.

"But you missed the balloon."

"I'm so sorry," said Christopher Robin,

and he fired again.

This time he hit the balloon,

and the air came slowly out,

and Winnie-the-Pooh

floated down to the ground.

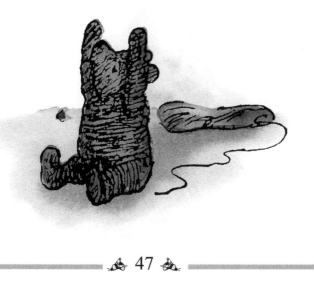

But his arms were so stiff

from holding the balloon all that time

that they stayed straight in the air

for more than a week.

And whenever a fly came

and settled on his nose,

he had to blow it off.

And I think—but I am not sure—

that *that* is why

he was always called Pooh.